It's going to be
a spooky summer!

"My name is Robert Campbell," said the glowing man. "I was a counselor here in 1941."

I looked at him closely. He was young and kind of handsome. He had a square jaw, a straight nose, and big eyes. But no color. No color at all. I held on to my theory that he was a holographic projection.

"You weren't even born in 1941," I said.

"Stand still!" said Robert. His voice was very powerful. He put his hand on my chest. Then he put his hand *through* my chest.

Books by Bruce Coville

Aliens Ate My Homework
The Dragonslayers
Goblins in the Castle
Monster of the Year

Camp Haunted Hills:
  How I Survived My Summer Vacation
  Some of My Best Friends Are Monsters
  The Dinosaur That Followed Me Home

Magic Shop Books:
  Jennifer Murdley's Toad
  Jeremy Thatcher, Dragon Hatcher
  The Monster's Ring

My Teacher Books:
  My Teacher Is an Alien
  My Teacher Fried My Brains
  My Teacher Glows in the Dark
  My Teacher Flunked the Planet

Space Brat Books:
  Space Brat
  Space Brat 2: Blork's Evil Twin
  Space Brat 3: The Wrath of Squat

Available from MINSTREL Books

How I Survived
My Summer Vacation

by
Bruce Coville

Illustrated by
Tom Newsom

A GLC Book

PUBLISHED BY POCKET BOOKS

New York   London   Toronto   Sydney   Tokyo   Singapore

**For my brother, Robert,
another goodhearted wiseguy**

This book is a work of fiction. Names, characters, places and incidents are
either the product of the author's imagination or are used fictitiously. Any
resemblance to actual events or locales or persons, living or dead, is entirely
coincidental.

A MINSTREL PAPERBACK *ORIGINAL*

A Minstrel Book published by
POCKET BOOKS, a division of Simon & Schuster Inc.
1230 Avenue of the Americas, New York, NY 10020

Special thanks to Pat MacDonald, Robin Stevenson,
and Gwendolyn Smith.

Cover art and illustrations by Tom Newsom
Book design by Alex Jay/Studio J
Mechanicals by Mary LeCleir
Typesetting by David E. Scham Associates Inc.
Developed by Byron Preiss and Daniel Weiss
Editor: Ruth Ashby

ISBN: 0-671-68176-1

First Minstrel Books printing June 1988

11 12 13 14 15 16 17 18 19 20

A MINSTREL BOOK and colophon are registered trademarks
of Simon & Schuster Inc.

"Camp Haunted Hills" is a trademark of
General Licensing Company, Inc.

Printed in the U.S.A.

Chapter One

Bus Ride to Doom

Sure, I know you've heard of Camp Haunted Hills. Who hasn't, now that the movie's such a hit?

But let me tell you—what you saw in your local theater is not exactly what happened.

I know, because I was there. My name is Stuart Glassman, and I was a camper at Haunted Hills that first summer, back when Gregory Stevens was still keeping the place fairly secret. And as much as I like the movie, the truth is, it's mostly Hollywood baloney. Oh, sure, the creature and the ghost were both there. But not the way you saw them. Take the creature: in real life, I doubt she was more than seven feet tall. And as for the ghost—well, we'll get to Robert later.

For now, just believe me: if you want to understand what went on at Camp Haunted Hills that summer, forget everything you think you know.

Because I'm about to tell you what really happened—creatures, ghost, and all.

If I didn't love movies so much, I probably never would have gotten mixed up in all this. But I do. I mean, I saw *Battle for the Galaxy* fifteen times— the first week it was playing!

My poor parents think I'm pretty weird. They used to worry about it, until they looked around and realized every kid they knew was weird. After a while they decided there were worse things than wanting to direct films when you grow up. As my father said to my mother one night, "Look at it this way, Louise. There's weird, and there's weird. At least Stuart doesn't want to be president!"

Anyway, loving movies the way I do, when I spotted that little ad for Camp Haunted Hills on the funnies page of our local paper, I knew I *had* to go. I had friends who had gone to tennis camps and computer camps and even fat camps. But I had never even heard of a *movie* camp. So I wrote off for the information. When the brochure came I took it to my parents, threw myself on the floor, grabbed their feet, and pleaded with them to send me off to camp.

As soon as they said yes, I started to wonder what I had gotten myself into. I mean, we were talking about eight weeks in a strange place—Ore-

2

gon. I'd never been away from home for more than an overnight before. I still slept with a night-light and a teddy bear. (Oh, stop laughing. I happen to know that there are a lot of eleven-year-olds who still have teddy bears.) But I knew I couldn't take Igor—that's my bear—to camp. Suddenly, going away didn't seem like such a good idea after all. What was I supposed to do?

I was still trying to figure that out four months later when my parents took me to meet the camp bus. "I think maybe I should stay home after all," I said just before they pushed me into line to board the bus. "Jeremiah will probably miss me."

Jeremiah is our golden retriever. He's not very bright. Actually, I figured if I stayed away for over a week he was more likely to forget me than miss me. I could just see him wandering into my room and looking around with that vague expression of his. "I think someone used to live here," he would say to himself. Then he'd go wag his tail and knock something off the coffee table. He's that kind of dog.

"Jeremiah will be fine," said my father. Dad is big on having me finish whatever I start. I was beginning to think he only agreed to send me to camp because he knew I'd change my mind and he thought it would be fun to watch me try to squirm my way out of it. He's that kind of father.

3

Five minutes later I was sitting in the bus with my face pressed against the window. I hoped if I looked pathetic enough my parents would change their minds and rescue me. My mother's lower lip started to tremble. I was getting to her! Then my father put his arm around her and whispered in her ear, and I knew he had decided to be strong for both of them. I was sunk.

And right then, just when I thought things were as bad as they could get, a girl came and sat down next to me.

A girl, for pete's sake! An almost pudgy girl with a big smile and long brown braids. "Hi!" she said. "My name's Brenda Connors. What's yours?"

I groaned and sank back in my seat. Life is hard enough when you're skinny and wear thick glasses and you're being shipped off to camp without your bear. When I had that much going against me already, I didn't need a girl sitting next to me on the camp bus. Socially speaking, I figured I was ruined.

An hour after we left my home in northern California, I started getting bus sick. I wondered if the embarrassment of throwing up might be balanced out if I could manage to do it on Brenda.

Two hours after we left the city and were well up in the mountains, I realized that until then I didn't know what bus sick was all about. *Now* I was bus sick. I thought I would rather die than drive another mile like this.

Three hours after we left the city, I was looking out the window when suddenly the bus screeched left, then right. It was incredible. One minute we were rolling along the pavement. The next, we shot over the edge of the road and were hanging in mid-air, a hundred feet above a raging river filled with jagged rocks.

Chapter Two

"Expect the Unexpected!"

For the first time I understood what people mean when they say, "My heart was in my throat." I also know how it happens. It's because your stomach is pushing from behind, trying to beat it to the exit.

All around me I heard people screaming. Kids threw their arms around one another and held on, waiting for the end. I wondered if my parents would miss me when I was gone.

The whole thing lasted about three seconds. That's not how long it took to hit bottom; it's how long it took to figure out that the bus wasn't really falling. In fact, it seemed as if we were flying, as we floated across the gap in the mountains and landed gently on a road on the opposite side.

It was great to realize we weren't going to die, until I noticed I had my arms around Brenda Connors. "Yow!" I screamed, wondering if I was happy about surviving after all.

Everyone on the bus started jabbering about what had just happened, how exciting it was, and how scared they had been.

Well, almost everyone. The kid sitting behind me just said, "What's the big deal? I knew what it was about all along." I found out later that his name was Lucius Colton. Lucius is about half a foot taller than I am. His family has *money*. He wears mirror sunglasses. He thinks the only thing cooler than he is was the last Ice Age. As far as I'm concerned he's about as much fun as a trip to the dentist.

It's possible Lucius was telling the truth when he said he knew what was going on. For my part, I think it was more fun to be fooled.

"Attention please. Attention please!" said the driver through his microphone. Even as excited as we were, we began to quiet down. Everyone was dying to know what he was going to say. But he didn't say anything. He just opened the door.

A dark-haired man climbed the steps and smiled at us. I closed my eyes. What I was seeing wasn't possible. But when I opened my eyes the man was still there.

"Hello," he said. "My name is Gregory Stevens, and I want to welcome you to Camp Haunted Hills."

It *was* him. I couldn't believe it! I, Stuart Glass-

8

man, was on a bus with the man who had directed *Battle for the Galaxy*. Suddenly I wondered if the bus really had crashed. This sure felt like heaven!

"I hope you enjoyed our little welcome," said Mr. Stevens. "We wanted you to know we weren't kidding when we said 'Expect the unexpected!' That's what Camp Haunted Hills is all about, and it's just a taste of the surprises we've planned for you this summer."

A tall blond man stepped up behind Mr. Stevens. "This is Peter Flinches. You'll see a lot of him— he's in charge of Camp Haunted Hills."

"What about you, Mr. Stevens?" yelled someone behind me.

"Oh, I'll be around," he said with a grin. "But I'm pretty busy in Hollywood right now. In case you haven't heard, we start filming the third episode of *Battle for the Galaxy* next week."

The bus broke into wild cheering, everybody clapping and stamping and whistling. Mr. Stevens smiled. "Wait till you see it!" he yelled. "It'll knock your socks off!"

And then he was gone. He didn't disappear in a puff of smoke, or anything like that. He was just— gone. I still don't know if it was some kind of special effect, or if he just moved fast.

Peter Flinches made a short speech, welcoming us to the camp and talking about what we would be doing for the summer. "Now settle back and enjoy the rest of your ride," he said. "In forty-five minutes you'll be at camp. Your counselors will be waiting with your bunk assignments."

He stepped off the bus and we started rolling. Twisting around in my seat, I looked through the back window. I could see an arrangement of cables and pulleys stretching from cliff to cliff. I figured we had been carried across the gap by something like the giant tow lifts that carry groups of people up a mountainside.

I also saw Gregory Stevens standing in the road and looking back in the direction we had come.

The next bus was just rounding the corner.

"Boy," I thought. "Are those guys in for a surprise."

We rolled on, past trees as big around as houses. After a while we turned onto a dirt road, and that's when I really learned what bus sick was all about.

"Feel better?" Brenda asked when I staggered back from the restroom.

I nodded.

"That's funny," said Lucius. "You look worse. I think it's the green in your cheeks."

I sank back into my seat. *It's going to be a long summer*, I thought.

Five hundred years later we pulled through the

camp gates. A group of college-age people was waiting for us. Everyone was dressed in shorts and Camp Haunted Hills T-shirts. I liked the T-shirts. On the front they had a picture of a ghost and the words *Camp Haunted Hills.* On the back they said, *Home of Tomorrow's Greatest Filmmakers.*

Noise. Confusion. Yelling. It was just like the school cafeteria. Suddenly I heard my name. I crossed to a small group of boys about my age. They were clustered around a tall redhead who carried a clipboard and wore a whistle around his neck.

Standing next to him was Lucius Colton.

"Hi, geek," said Lucius.

I felt the summer had just gotten six weeks longer.

Once the counselor had found all of us, he told us his name was Dan and that he would show us our bunks.

We hadn't gone far from the parking lot when I spotted a skinny guy walking through the woods a little way from us. He had curly brown hair and a big nose. He also had a huge lizard sitting on his shoulder.

When he heard us walking by, the guy turned in our direction. "Look, Myron," he said to the lizard, holding it in front of him. "Fresh meat!"

11

"What a geek!" said Lucius.

"Who was that?" I asked, running to catch up with Dan.

"His name's Harry Housen," said Dan. "He's part of the film staff. I'd stay away from him if I were you. He's pretty weird."

Personally I'm in favor of weird people. But before I could say anything in Harry's defense, we had reached the bunkhouse.

"Here it is, gentlemen," said Dan, throwing open the door of a small building made of slabs of wood still covered with bark. "Your home for the next eight weeks."

As I was walking through the door, I remembered a question I had wanted to ask ever since I'd first read about the camp.

"Hey, Dan," I said, pausing halfway into the bunkhouse. "Why do they call this place Camp Haunted Hills, anyway?"

"I don't know," he said, giving me a little push to get me moving again. "I suppose it's because of the ghost."

Chapter Three

A Shark Named Seymour

Four sets of bunk beds took up about half the space in the little building. Since I was the fifth one through the door, the top bunks were already taken. I threw my stuff on the bottom bunk near the back wall, which seemed like the best spot available, until I realized I was under Lucius.

I looked around, wondering if any of the other kids would make good friends. I also wondered which ones were most likely to pick on me. The kid directly across from me had dark hair, a ton of freckles, and a round face. His name was Eddie Mayhew. I saw a *Captain Crusher* comic jammed in his backpack and decided he'd probably be a good bet for a friend.

Before I could say anything to Eddie, Dan blew his whistle and yelled, "Into your swimsuits! We're going to the waterfront for your swimming tests."

That was fine with me. I'm a terrific swimmer.

I looked for the changing room. There wasn't any. What was I supposed to do—change right here in front of everyone? Now I *knew* this had been a stupid idea. I dug out my trunks, then sat on the bed and changed as quickly as I could.

At the waterfront we were met by a black man wearing a red bathing suit and a whistle. He was only a few inches taller than I am, but his muscles had muscles.

"They're all yours, Splash!" said Dan. Then he took off as if he was afraid "Splash" might tell him to take us back.

The waterfront man blew his whistle and told us to line up. Another whistle! I wondered if one of the tests for being a camp counselor was how loud and long you could blow your whistle.

He told us his name was Splash Calhoun. Then he set us up for *our* tests. I was taking the Dolphin Test, which was for the best swimmers. Three other guys, including Lucius and Eddie, lined up to take it with me. After I dove in and surfaced, I shook my hair back and my eyes popped open wide. Slicing through the water, straight at me, was a huge black fin!

"Shark!" I screamed, scrambling back up on the dock. "Shark!"

I was not amused when the fin stopped at the dock and the tall, lean man who was wearing it on his

14

back climbed out of the water. Well, I'm not entirely stupid. I know sharks don't live in freshwater lakes in Oregon. But when you see something like that, you react first and think later.

Lucius, on the other hand, was incredibly amused. In fact, he was almost sick with laughing.

I was so upset with myself for falling for the joke that I forgot one of the reasons I had wanted to come to Camp Haunted Hills was for the thrills and chills.

The man with the fin turned out to be Splash's assistant, Flipper. He was blond and tan. He would have been movie-star handsome, except for two things: he had a goofy grin and ears like tent flaps. I liked him almost instantly, in spite of the fact that he had just made a fool of me. Anyone who grins like that can't be all bad.

"Well, boys," said Flipper, taking off the strap that held the fin to his back. "Now that it's safe to go back in, are you ready to take your tests?"

I nodded and the three guys lined up behind me again. Just as we were about to dive in, an enormous shark burst out of the water three feet in front of us.

This was no man with a fin. This was a shark with a head like a Volkswagen, eyes like death, and teeth like spearheads. We staggered back, screaming. Even Lucius seemed terrified.

Flipper was holding a lifeguard's pole. He rapped the shark across the head. "Scram, Seymour!" he shouted.

Seymour!

Even though my heart was pounding against my ribs as if it was looking for an escape route, my brain finally remembered four things:

1) Sharks don't live in freshwater lakes.

2) Gregory Steven's first big hit was *White Death*—the ultimate shark movie.

3) The pet name for the mechanical shark in that film was Seymour.

4) In a Gregory Stevens production it was *never* safe to go back in the water.

I felt better about falling for this shark, since everyone else had, too. Actually, the funniest thing that afternoon was watching Lucius try to pretend he *hadn't* been scared. He reminded me of a cat who falls off a chair while it's asleep, and then tries to pretend it did it on purpose.

Flipper was standing at the edge of the dock, poking his lifeguard pole into the water. "You just settle down, Seymour!" he yelled. "No one likes a smart-aleck fish!"

Then he jumped on the shark's back. I don't care if Seymour was mechanical. It was incredibly neat to swim with the lifeguard traveling beside me on a giant shark. It was worth a few scares.

I passed the test and got my Dolphin tag. Dan showed up about the time we were done to take us back to our bunk.

Along the way I spotted a huge footprint beside the trail. Not just big. HUGE. And it looked like a human print—not an animal one. I could put both my feet inside it—end to end or side by side. They fit either way.

My first reaction was to laugh. After two fake sharks, I was getting used to this kind of stuff. They could only fool me so many times. The other kids gathered around it, too. We all got a big kick out of it. (Get it? Big kick?)

The weird thing was, Dan didn't seem to think it was funny. He got a strange look on his face. For a minute I felt frightened again. Maybe this wasn't a camp joke. Maybe it was something else.

Then I realized that in a movie camp a lot of the counselors were sure to be out-of-work actors. I knew young actors were always taking odd jobs while they waited for their big break. I figured most of them would love to work for Gregory Stevens— even at a summer camp.

So I figured Dan was pretending that he didn't know anything about the footprint. It was just part of the game.

Which just goes to show you how wrong a guy can be.

Chapter Four

What Did Eddie See?

One way Camp Haunted Hills was like a Gregory Stevens movie, at least on the first day, was that we never had time to catch our breath. When we got back from the waterfront, we finished getting settled in. Then it was off to the mess hall for dinner.

The tables were set up to hold ten people—eight campers and two counselors. They were arranged boy, girl, boy, girl—that is, there was a table of girls next to every table of boys.

But at each table there were both a male and a female counselor. Dan sat with us, of course. We wondered who our female staff member would be.

We didn't wait long to find out. Shortly after we had taken our places, a woman with long blond hair, big green eyes, and a figure like Miss America's walked up to the table and said, "Excuse me, but is this where Bunk Thirteen sits?"

"It certainly is," said Dan, jumping up and knocking over his chair in the process.

The woman smiled. "Then this is where I belong."

I had to admire Dan. From the look in his eye, he wanted to get down on his knees and offer a prayer of thanks. Instead he picked up his chair and said, "You must be from the film staff. I don't think we've met."

"Right on both counts," she said. "I'm the makeup specialist. My name is Aurora Jackson." She glanced down the table and smiled. "Makeup's a good speciality to have," she said. "You'd never know it, but I'm really short, fat, and ugly."

We all laughed. I looked at her and thought, *If she's really ugly, then I'm King Kong.*

We went around the table and introduced ourselves. I had an urge to stand up and say, "My name is Stuart Glassman, and I'd do anything for you because you're the most beautiful woman I've ever seen." Fortunately, I was able to resist. The world does enough to make me feel foolish; I don't need to help it along.

Aurora smiled and called us all by name. I wondered if the other guys were melting inside, too. It was a relief when the waiters showed up with the food.

Like everything else at Camp Haunted Hills, the

food was a little different. Instead of beans and franks, we had this fancy chicken where they had taken out the bones and rolled the meat around other stuff.

"Ick! What is this?" cried Eddie Mayhew when he cut his open and the goo starting oozing out.

"Chicken *cordon bleu*," said Aurora, slicing a dainty bite off her own serving.

"Don't worry," said Dan. "This is a welcome-to-camp dinner. Tomorrow night you get normal slop, like in every other camp."

Aurora rolled her eyes. I could have watched her do that all night. Unfortunately, my concentration was interrupted by a finger in my ribs. I turned around and saw a smiling face surrounded by two brown pigtails.

"Hi, Stuart," said Brenda. "How's it going?"

She was going to be at the table right behind me—three times a day! How unlucky can a guy get?

"It's going fine," I said, and turned back to my plate quickly, so nobody would get the idea she was my girlfriend—or anything stupid like that.

Aside from Brenda, I really enjoyed that meal. The food was great, even if it was weird. Aurora and Dan were really funny. And after an incredible dessert (white cake, chocolate ice cream, fresh strawberries and orange sauce), Peter Flinches, the

21

camp director, announced that we were going to see a short film. He pressed a button. A huge screen rolled down from the ceiling. Another button sent heavy black curtains snapping over the windows. A third button and the lights went out. The mess hall was also a movie theater!

I know—lots of camps show movies. But how many of them use 70-millimeter projectors with Dolby stereo? A burst of music filled the dining hall. "WELCOME TO CAMP HAUNTED HILLS!" said the screen in letters five feet tall.

Suddenly Gregory Stevens appeared on the screen. He was sitting at an editing machine, looking at some film. He glanced up, as if we had just walked into the room. "Hello!" he said. "It's good to see you again. I hope you've enjoyed your first day at Camp Haunted Hills."

He stepped away from the machine. "I created Camp Haunted Hills because I love movies—and because I remember what it was like to love movies and not know how to get started making them.

"If *you* want to learn to make movies, too, then you've come to the right place."

I almost jumped out of my skin. All my fears about the camp disappeared. Because there is nothing, *nothing* I want to do more than make movies.

Gregory continued speaking. "Another reason I

started Camp Haunted Hills was to provide a place where talented young filmmakers—the staff here—could practice their special-effects skills for the kinds of films we want to make."

He stepped closer to the camera. "But do you know the main reason I started this camp?"

He looked to one side, and then to the other, as if it was some terrific secret. Then he leaned forward. "The real reason," he whispered, "is that I thought it would be fun!"

Everybody began cheering.

After the film, the staff stood up and introduced themselves. It turned out that weird Harry Housen was the special-effects teacher. He still had his pet iguana, Myron, on his shoulder. He also stuttered a little when he talked.

"What a geek!" whispered Lucius.

I didn't care. I loved special effects more than anything. I was determined to get to know Harry Housen.

Then we marched up to the campfire grounds. After what I've told you about this place, you can imagine what that campfire was like. First, the fire lit itself, with blue flames that shot about twenty feet into the air. Then halfway through our second song a witch appeared—seemingly out of nowhere—and tried to cast a spell on us. Three of the staff members tried to stop her, and it turned into one of the funniest skits I've ever seen. Buckets of water got thrown everywhere. Before it was over the performers were completely soaked. So were most of the kids in the first three rows. My sides hurt from laughing.

Well, by the time we were ready to go to sleep that night, we were pretty used to the kinds of tricks Camp Haunted Hills was throwing at us. So when Eddie Mayhew went out to use the latrine, and came running back screaming that he had seen a ghost, all we did was laugh.

"Honest, you guys!" he said. "I saw him. For real!"

His face was so white, his freckles looked as if they were going to fall right off it.

"Sure, Eddie," said Lucius. "And it wasn't a counselor in white makeup, or a hologram, or a robot, or anything else like that. Just a real-live-dead person."

Eddie blushed. "I saw what I saw," he said.

I had to admire Eddie. It took a lot of nerve to stand up to Lucius's sarcasm.

About two o'clock in the morning I woke up and realized I had to take a leak. Suddenly I remembered the look in Eddie's eyes and what he had said.

"I saw what I saw."

Just what did *he see?* I wondered, while I lay

there trying to talk myself out of having to go to the bathroom. It was hopeless. The more I told myself I didn't need to go, the worse it got. Finally I gave in and got up.

Fishing out my flashlight from under my pillow, I headed for the door. I remembered the special-effects surprises at the swimming test and the campfire.

Please, I thought, *at least let me go to the bathroom in peace.*

Then I gathered my courage and opened the door.

Chapter Five

The Haunted Outhouse

A light rain was falling. It made the night pleasantly cool. I heard frogs croaking beside the lake, the breeze rustling through the treetops, wings fluttering nearby. I tried to remember whether or not you could hear bats fly.

Swinging my flashlight around, I found the path to the latrine. Once I was in the woods I barely felt the rain, though I could hear it pattering on the leaves above me. Even so, the ground was wet enough to make me wish I had taken time to put on my sneakers. Something scurried through the bushes beside me. I wondered about my toes. I remembered my father telling me that when he was in the Peace Corps in South America, they had to cover their feet at night to keep the vampire bats off their toes. I didn't think Oregon had vampire bats. But I wasn't certain.

In case you've never been there, let me explain

that when you're out in the woods at two o'clock in the morning it's easy to spook yourself. You can believe almost anything. You start to *expect* almost anything. So I was relieved when I got to the latrine and nothing jumped out at me.

I went inside and did my business.

I came out and started back down the path.

"Feel better?" asked a voice behind me.

I made a very intelligent reply—something like "Aaaahhhh!" I didn't know if I should turn around or run like crazy. I started to run, but caught myself, remembering how we had all laughed at Eddie. I didn't want to get the same treatment. Besides, I knew it was just another Camp Haunted Hills trick. So I gathered my nerve for the second time that night and turned back to the latrine.

A glowing figure stood on top of the little building. He began to applaud. "Very good," he said. "Much better than the last little wimp that came out here."

I had to admit they didn't do anything halfway at Camp Haunted Hills. This was the most realistic ghost I had ever seen. I wondered whether it was one of the counselors in glowing white makeup, or some kind of superadvanced holographic projection.

The ghost spoke again. "Aren't you afraid of me?"

I studied him for a minute. His feet straddled the peak of the little roof. He had his hands on his hips and a mocking smile on his face. Although he was in the open, I couldn't see his features very clearly because of the rain and his own slight glow. Yet somehow he seemed friendly.

"I probably would be afraid of you," I said, "if you weren't just a trick."

He stepped off the roof and floated to the ground. "What do you mean, trick? What's going on around here, anyway?"

I swallowed. He was getting more believable by the minute. But I remembered the flying bus, the shark, the witch at the campfire, and kept my cool.

"That was very impressive," I said.

"It's one of the first things you learn."

"In special-effects class?"

"Well, they don't really call it that," he said. "They don't really call it anything. After you die you just find you can float around if you want to."

"Cute," I said.

The glowing man looked puzzled. "Are we talking about the same thing?"

"I don't know. I'm talking about being a counselor. What are you talking about?"

"Being a ghost."

I thought the joke had gone on too long. "Come on," I said. "You're no ghost, you're a counselor.

You know it. I know it. You know I know it. So why not drop the act?"

"I used to be a counselor," he said. "But that was a long time ago—back before I died."

Obviously he wasn't going to let go of the gag. But I was tired, cold, and worried about the slimy things I seemed to feel around my feet. "Look," I said, "I need some sleep. I'll see you around."

I turned and headed back down the path.

He hurried to catch up to me. "Geez, kid," he asked, "what does it take to convince you?"

I yawned.

He walked through a tree.

I stopped dead in my tracks. "How did you do that?"

"I'm a ghost, dummy!"

I looked at him more closely and realized I could see right through him. I started to get scared again. Part of me wanted to run. But another part of me was convinced that the minute I did, a dozen counselors would fall out of the bushes, laughing like crazy.

I didn't want to be laughed at. I also didn't want to stand in the woods in the middle of the night with a spook.

"My name is Robert Campbell," said the glowing man. "I was a counselor here in 1941."

I looked at him more closely. He was young and

kind of handsome. He had a square jaw, a straight nose, and big eyes. But no color. No color at all. I held onto my theory that he was a holographic projection.

"You weren't even born in 1941," I said.

"Stand still!" said Robert. His voice was very powerful. He put his hand on my chest. Then he put his hand *through* my chest. That was all right. It was possible with a hologram, if it was good enough.

What wasn't all right was the terrible cold that went tunneling through me. I felt as if every bit of warmth was being sucked out of me—as though I had been shoved out of the house on a winter day with no clothes on.

No hologram could do that.

My eyes went wide. "You really *are* a ghost!"

"That's what I've been trying to tell you."

I screamed and ran down the path. I didn't use my flashlight. I didn't care where I stepped. I just wanted to get out of there.

I heard a cold, strange laugh behind me and ran even faster. When I reached the bunk I threw open the door, barreled across the floor, and dove under my blanket. I stayed there for the rest of the night, afraid to close my eyes.

Chapter Six

The Ghost Who Wouldn't Shut Up

By morning I had almost convinced myself that Robert was only a holographic projection after all. It was hard to believe the staff could create something that realistic. But the alternative—that I had really seen a ghost—was even harder to swallow.

All through breakfast I expected some counselor to come up and make a sly comment about my reaction to the "ghost." Everyone would have a big laugh at my expense, but I would finally be sure it was only a joke. I was almost looking forward to it.

But things didn't work out the way I expected. No one said a thing about the ghost—even when I dropped a couple of hints to Dan during the meal. Then, shortly after we finished eating, Robert himself showed up and gave me my first taste of what it would be like to have a ghost for a friend. Not that I had any intention of being his friend, mind you. But he seemed to have picked me out for special attention. A few days later when I asked him why, he just shrugged and said, "You're the weirdest kid here. I figure you need all the friends you can get."

Robert was incredibly rude, even for a ghost.

Anyway, we had just finished eating. A skinny lady with frizzy hair had bounded to the front of the room. "Good morning, campers!" she said cheerfully. "My name is Wanda Danns, and I'm the Camp Haunted Hills social director. It's my job to make *sure* you have fun all summer long!"

That was when Robert made his appearance. He drifted down through the roof, then stood beside Wanda, making funny faces. I broke out laughing. I thought everyone else would get a kick out of this, too. But no one did. In fact, everyone at my table looked at me as if I was a complete moron. Aurora shot me a nasty glance and told me to be quiet. Lucius snickered, but it was clear he was laughing at me and not at Robert. Even Eddie Mayhew didn't seem to see him.

The hair along the back of my scalp began to stand up.

I had been willing to believe that a holographic projection could do the incredible things I had seen last night. I wasn't willing to believe they had invented a hologram that only I could see. Which left only one other explanation: *Robert Campbell was really a ghost.*

I thought about screaming. But I had already made myself look foolish enough for one morning. Besides, seeing a ghost in broad daylight, with a hundred other people around, isn't quite as scary as seeing one by yourself in the middle of the night. So I held my ground and waited to see what Robert would do next.

What he did was come to visit me. He walked down the center aisle, smiling and waving like some kind of movie star. Then, when he got to our table, he floated into the air, drifted over the plates, and sat down cross-legged about three inches above the remains of my eggs.

"Mornin', cowboy," he said in a hearty voice.

"Be quiet!" I hissed.

He had done it again! Dan reached around Eddie Mayhew and flicked me on the ear. "*You* be quiet!" he said, his voice low but firm.

I resolved not to say anything else to Robert, no matter how he tempted me.

It wasn't easy. He had a wisecrack for everything anyone else said or did. "It's too bad about her hair," he said, gesturing at Wanda. "But then, I've noticed that terrible things have happened to women's hair since I died."

I started to laugh but caught myself so that it

34

only came out as a little snort through my nose. I was going to have to watch it. If Robert did that to me while I was drinking milk it could be disastrous. One of the worst moments of my life had come from laughing milk through my nose when I was in third grade. It's incredibly embarrassing. And it hurts.

It wasn't easy to pay attention to Wanda with Robert chattering away, but her basic message was that after breakfast everyone was supposed to go to the recreation hall to sign up for the first two weeks of courses.

"You know, I don't even know your name," said Robert as we were leaving the dining hall. "What is it?"

"Stuart," I said, before I could stop myself.

"Oh, great," said Lucius, who was walking to my left. "Not only is he a geek—he talks to himself. You are truly weird, Glassman."

"Now see what you made me do," I said to Robert, which only made Lucius think I was even weirder.

"Ignore him," said Robert. "He's a creep."

I didn't have to be told that; I had it figured out when I met Lucius on the bus. But I wasn't about to say that to Robert. I wasn't about to say *anything* else to him if I could manage it.

The staff had set up booths in the rec hall so

that people could go around and sign up for things like acting and makeup and lighting design and costuming. I was interested in special effects, of course, and I was afraid there would be a long line at Harry Housen's booth.

As it turned out, the line wasn't as long as I'd expected. Lucius, who was standing ahead of me— did you expect him to be behind me?—said there would be more people if Harry wasn't such a geek.

"Doesn't that boy know any other word?" asked Robert.

I tried to glare him into silence, but even that turned out to be a problem, since a girl in the next line thought I was looking at her and glared back angrily.

"Will you please leave me alone?" I said, mouthing the words but not saying them aloud.

"Of course not," said Robert cheerfully. "I like you!"

We were almost at the front of the line now. Harry was sitting behind the table, looking sort of lost and mournful. I noticed that he didn't have his iguana on is shoulder.

"Where's Myron?" I asked, to let him know that I had been paying attention to him, and that unlike most people, I didn't think he was weirder than real-life.

"Missing," said Harry glumly. "When I woke up this morning the top of his cage was loose, and he was gone." He sighed. "I'm worried about the little fella."

"I'm sorry," I said, putting my name on his list. "But I bet he'll show up before long."

"I don't know," said Harry glumly. "He's never been out on his own before. I'm afraid he won't know where home is."

I glanced back at Harry as I left the table. He looked as if he had lost his best friend. When I thought about it, I decided he probably had.

The first thing on my schedule that morning was a swimming lesson. "I hate the water," said Robert as he watched me get out my trunks. "I'll see you later."

Then he vanished, just the way the picture on a television disappears when you turn it off.

My first thought was "Good, I'm glad he's gone." But after a few minutes I realized I actually missed his stream of silly chatter.

The waterfront was a little more calm that morning: I had my entire swimming lesson without a single interruption from sharks, submarines, or monster octopuses—none of which would have surprised me at this point.

After swimming, I had a free half hour, which I

spent talking about Captain Crusher with Eddie Mayhew. Then I headed for the first of the day's two sessions with Harry.

On the way to the special-effects shop I had a daydream about getting to be really good friends with Harry. In my fantasy Harry was amazed by my understanding of special effects. He decided I had a real gift for them and offered to teach me everything he knew. It was great!

Harry's workshop was in a large wooden building surrounded by enormous pine trees. It was located about a quarter of a mile from the waterfront. As I hurried along the path, I noticed another one of those huge footprints just off the trail.

In all, twenty people had signed up for Harry's class. My heart sank. How could I get him to notice me with all these other people around? How could I make him understand that I loved special effects more than anyone in the room did except him?

Chapter Seven

Missing—One Iguana

"Stop!" yelled Harry.

We had been milling around, getting ready to sit down. Harry's unexpected shout froze us where we stood.

"Good," he said. "Now don't move until I say so."

He raised his hand. He was holding a black cylinder with a button on one end. A long black wire dangled from the other end, disappearing under his desk. He pushed the button. I heard a faint *click*.

"All right," said Harry, "everyone lift your right hand three inches."

We looked at one another, but did as he said.

Another *click*.

"Now do it again."

He went on like this for a minute or so, leading us through a series of actions. Then he asked us to sit down.

We sat. The lights went out. A screen lowered from the ceiling. The next thing we knew, it was filled with a film of us kids moving in strange and jerky ways. The way our hands seemed to fly across the screen was hilarious.

"Movies are just a series of images," said Harry, turning on the lights. "You show one picture after another, and the eye blends them together. Movies fool the eye. Special effects fool it even more."

Then he set us working in groups of three to make a short film with stop-motion animation. To do this you take a picture of something, move the something a tiny bit, take another picture, move the thing again, shoot it, move it, shoot it, move it, and so on. When it's shown on a screen, the images blend together and the thing looks as if it's really moving. You can show anything from a chair sliding across the floor by itself to a battle between little clay monsters that look like giants when they're blown up on the movie screen.

I always get nervous when I have to team up with someone. Fortunately, the kids I ended up with—a tall, skinny black kid named Keith Carter and an oriental girl named Melinda Chang—were pretty neat. Actually, that made sense; anyone who likes special effects can't be all bad. All right, so there's Lucius. But my mother always says there's an exception to every rule. He proves it.

Brenda was in the class, too, which didn't exactly thrill me.

"These cameras are old," said Harry, when each group had found a work space. "The new ones are much more sophisticated. Even so, these are a hundred times better than anything I learned on."

"The magic touch of Gregory Stevens," whispered Melinda.

"The magic touch of money!" Keith grinned. Somehow he managed to say it in a way that was funny, without being nasty. I thought maybe I should introduce him to Lucius. Maybe his style would rub off.

"To animate something means to bring it to life," said Harry, dumping a huge box full of stuff onto the big table in the center of the room. "What I want you to do is pick something out of this pile and figure out how it would move if it were alive."

Our team finally settled on three red rubber balls and a set of jacks. After some more instruction from Harry, we started working.

After lunch we picked up right where we had left off. It was slow work but a lot of fun. Once when we were stuck I just stood there looking around the room. It was a wonderful place, cluttered with cameras and sound equipment and mysterious boxes covered with lights and switches and dials. My fingers itched to get hold of them and find out what they were all about. The walls were covered with posters from great science fiction and fantasy movies. Microphones hung from the ceiling. It was like being in heaven.

The only sad thing was Harry himself. Whenever he was helping someone he seemed lively and happy. But as soon as he was standing alone, his face would slip into a look of total tragedy. I knew it was because he was missing Myron.

The most mysterious thing about the workroom was a black door at the far end. It was held shut by an enormous padlock. "KEEP OUT! TOP SECRET!" was painted on it in huge red letters.

I was dying to know what was behind the door.

Robert showed up once during the afternoon session, but he just sort of floated over my shoulder without making too many rude comments, so I didn't mind. It was kind of nice, having a secret friend.

In fact, it was a terrific day—at least, until bedtime, when Lucius decided to use me for a demonstration of how to give a flying wedgie. I'm not going to describe it. But believe me, if anyone ever asks if you want one, say NO!

I was so exhausted by the time I finally climbed into my bunk that I didn't even bother changing into pajamas. That was when I felt it. Something scaly started slowly slithering up my leg.

Chapter Eight

"Keep Out! Top Secret!"

I screamed and jumped into the air. On the way down, I realized that the thing in my bed had to be Myron. I moved sideways to avoid squashing the poor critter and landed on the floor with a thud.

Everyone rushed to see what I was yelling about. When they say Myron, they fell over laughing.

"Makes sense," hooted Lucius from the top bunk. "If you were an iguana, wouldn't *you* head straight for Stuart?"

Myron just sat there blinking at us. All of a sudden I knew what I had to do.

"Keep laughing," I said, scooping him up and tucking him under my arm. "I'm taking Myron home."

"So long, Lizard Boy!" yelled Lucius as I walked out the door.

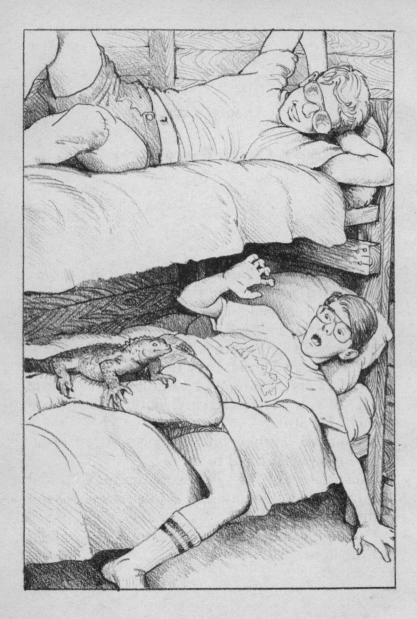

Robert shimmered into sight on the path just ahead of me.

"Well, aren't you going to thank me?" he asked.

"For what?"

"For talking Myron into crawling into your bunk."

"Thank you?" I yelled. "If you weren't dead, I could kill you. You scared me out of my skull. I'm lucky I didn't wet my pants."

"Well, sure," said Robert. "But you didn't want anyone else to find him, did you?"

I stopped. Of course I didn't want anyone else to find him. This was my golden chance to make friends with Harry.

"Well, thanks," I said grudgingly. "But the next time you decide to give me a hand, could you try to find a way that won't scare me to death?"

Robert shrugged. "What can I do? It's the ghost in me!"

By this time we had reached Harry's studio. I didn't know if he slept there or not, but I had a hunch he stayed up all hours working. He seemed the type.

I hoped I was right, because about then Myron decided he wanted to go for a walk on his own. "Hold still, Buster," I said, grabbing him behind the shoulders. Myron wasn't amused. He started thrashing back and forth. I grabbed his middle with my other hand and began yelling for Harry.

"Gee," said Robert, watching me struggle. "He wasn't like that when I talked to him this afternoon."

"You talked to him?" I gasped, between bellows.

"Sure," said Robert. "It's one of the advantages of being dead—you can talk to all kinds of things that you couldn't when you were alive. I remember when I was in Pago Pago—"

His story was cut off as Harry came bursting through the door. "Myron!" he cried. "You came back!"

"Not quite," I said, holding out both hands so Harry could take the thrashing lizard. "He had to be carried."

Harry was too thrilled by his reunion with Myron to pay much attention to me. He walked back into the building, scolding the iguana as he went. Myron stopped struggling. Harry set him on a table and began stroking him, all the time saying how worried he had been and what a bad iguana Myron was to run off like that.

Finally he noticed me standing there.

"Oh," he said as though he were seeing me for the first time. "I ought to thank you, uh—uh—"

My heart sank. He didn't even know my name!

"Stuart," I said. "Stuart Glassman. I'm in your class."

"Right!" said Harry. "I remember now. Well, thank you for bringing Myron home. Where did you find him?"

I explained how Myron had been in my bunk—though not how he had gotten there—and how I had jumped up, and how everyone had laughed at me.

Harry sighed. "I know what that's like," he said. From his voice I could tell he had been picked on himself. We got talking about being teased. Then we got talking about movies. That did it. Harry couldn't believe how many of his favorites I had seen, especially the old ones that a lot of people don't know about. He got us a couple of Cokes, carrying Myron on his shoulder as he went, and we settled in for a long movie talk.

Of course, a lot of the talk centered around special effects, and it didn't take long for Harry to figure out that I loved them almost as much as he did.

He looked at Myron, sitting on his shoulder.

He looked at me.

He seemed to make up his mind about something.

"Come here," he said. He led me to the black

door, the one that said "KEEP OUT! TOP SE-
CRET!" in huge red letters.

"I want to show you something." He looked
around nervously, as though he expected some in-
ternational spy to be listening. "Something incredible. It's my own project. When I perfect it, it's
going to change movies forever!"

He looked over his shoulder, then gestured for
me to follow him through the mysterious black
door.

Chapter Nine

Harry's Hologram

Harry's private workshop was about twelve feet wide and thirty feet long. An enormous table ran down the center of the room; two smaller workbenches lined the long walls. I had never seen so much neat stuff in one place in my whole life.

There were cameras all over, of course, and all kinds of other technical stuff—everything from component boards and reels of wire to dial-covered boxes big enough to hold a body.

If that had been all, it would have been interesting though not wonderful. But that wasn't all, because the room was devoted not only to special effects as science but to special effects as art. Everywhere I looked I saw model spaceships, miniature monsters, half-assembled masks, spare body parts, tubes and tubs of paint, and plaster and other assorted glop. A big vat under the table was labeled "Internal Organs" and a yellow five-gallon jug sitting nearby said "Fake Blood" in bright red letters. The walls were hung with feathers and fur and sheets of scaly stuff. A rack of background paintings of outer space and futuristic cities and undersea city ruins hung on the back wall. One end of the big table contained a miniature jungle."

"I've died and gone to heaven," I whispered.

"Don't be silly," said Robert. "Heaven is nothing like this."

"I suppose you know what it's like?" I said, forgetting that Harry was there.

"Of course," said Robert smugly.

"Yes, I do," said Harry, thinking I was talking to him. "I felt like that myself for the first time I walked into a special-effects shop."

"Well, I am impressed," said Robert. "If you can learn to answer me and still make sense to other people, our conversations should definitely improve."

I ignored him.

"So, do you want to see my project?" asked Harry. He rubbed his hands together in anticipation. His hair looked as if he had combed it with a fork. His eyes were gleaming. Except for the fact that he was at least twenty years too young, he would have made a wonderful mad scientist.

"Of course!" I said.

"Okay, help me move the big table."

He leaned against the big table. I looked at him doubtfully but took my place at the other end. To my surprise it slid easily across the floor.

"Hold it!" said Harry when we reached the workbench. He reached down and made some kind of adjustment. The whole table dropped down about twelve inches. One last push tucked it neatly under the workbench, leaving an enormous clear space in the center of the floor.

"Stand here," said Harry. He turned a knob on the wall. The lights grew dim. "Now watch!" he said triumphantly.

He flipped a switch. Something began to hum. Suddenly Myron was standing on the floor in front of me. Only it wasn't Myron. It was a holographic projection—the same kind of thing I thought Robert was when I first met him.

The image of the iguana looked right and left. Its tongue flicked out. I glanced at Harry. In the dim light I could see the real Myron sitting on his shoulder. If not for that, it would have been hard to believe what I saw on the floor wasn't the real thing.

At least that's what I thought until Harry started the next part of his show.

"Watch," he whispered as he turned on another dial. To my astonishment, the image on the floor doubled in size.

"Good Golly, Miss Molly," said Robert. "What won't they think of next?"

"Watch!" whispered Harry again, twisting the dial. Once more Myron's image doubled in size, making it nearly twice as big as me.

Robert slapped his forehead. "Jefferson Davis and my Aunt Mavis. What *does* he feed that boy?"

Before I could say anything, Harry turned the dial again. Suddenly Myron's image was sixteen feet long. His sides seemed to scrape the benches. I jumped backward. I knew it was only a projection. But it was a three-dimensional projection, it looked absolutely real, and it was staring me right in the face. I felt as if I could reach out and touch it. More important, I felt as if it could reach out and touch me—or swallow me, if it wanted to. I flinched as a tongue, as long as my arm and just as solid-looking flicked in my direction.

With a mad gleam in his eye, Harry twisted the dial one more time. For an instant I felt as if I was going to be crushed against the wall as the iguana expanded yet again. But Harry had pushed his machine to its limit. Suddenly the image became thin and ghostlike, even more transparent than Robert. Slowly it faded from sight.

"Phooey," said Harry. "That always happens when I get to the fifth level."

"But it's incredible," I said. "Absolutely amazing!"

"Do you really think so?"

I repeated myself, and we started talking about the ways it could be used in movies and amusement parks. The conversation went on half the night. I guess Harry must have felt pretty comfortable with me, because as secretive as he was, he finally told me about the special project he had in mind for our class.

I was so excited that even after I finally got back to my bunk, I stayed awake almost until dawn, thinking about what Harry had said.

Chapter Ten

Worlds of Wonder

The rest of that first week seemed to go by in a blur. I enjoyed the normal camp activities of swimming and softball and nature hiking. Meals were fun, especially because Aurora made herself look completely different for every supper; one night she'd have short blond hair and green eyes, the next night long dark hair and brown eyes.

It was also fun to watch Dan react to Aurora, since he seemed to have developed a terrible crush on her. She was always a little late. Then when she did show up, Dan would get flustered and do something like knock over his chair, pour bug juice in his lap, or drop his potatoes on the floor. I felt sorry for him. But since at least once a day Robert managed to trick me into talking to him when I shouldn't, it was a relief to have someone else act silly, too. It took some attention away from me.

As enjoyable as everything was, what I lived for

was special-effects class—or more specifically, the time when the class ended. That's because every day I hung around after the second session to spend my free time in Harry's back room, helping him with extra projects. We made little movies, experimenting with different techniques. I was his assistant, his model, his audience, and his "Gopher." (You know—"go for this, go for that.")

We spent one evening making a film of a frog climbing out of a hole in my arm. Disgusting! Another time Harry filmed me walking, then put the image over one of his background paintings, so it looked as if I was wandering around an undersea city. That was great. Secretly, I hoped I could work on a hologram. But that was his most private project, and he was keeping the technique under wraps.

I knew he was working on it, though, because a couple of times he showed me new images of Myron. Harry had a passion for dinosaurs, and he was always pasting wings or fins or some other disguise onto that poor lizard to make him look like a prehistoric creature. Once he even abandoned science for fantasy and made Myron look like a dragon; he covered the iguana with red makeup and figured out a way to make smoke come out of his nose. When he blew *that* image up sixteen feet long, the effect was absolutely terrifying.

One of Harry's goals was to make his projection

system simple enough to use almost anywhere. So the night after Myron made his first appearance as a dragon, we took the holo-projector outside. We climbed a tree to get the right height for our first open-air test.

"Incredible," I whispered to Harry, when Myron's image appeared beneath us. "I know it's only a trick with light. But I'd swear that was a real dragon down there."

"All you ever see is light," said Harry. "Light waves go into your eyes, and your brain turns them into pictures. So the right light can completely fool your eye—*and* your brain."

"Just like me," said Robert, floating up to sit on the branch beside me. "Nothing but thin air and a little light."

And a big mouth, I wanted to add. But I knew Harry would think I was talking to him.

Later Robert and I sat by the lake and talked for a while. I was feeling cranky with him because twice that day he had managed to trick me into saying something to him while other people were around.

"You know, I'm getting a reputation for being a real weirdo," I said. "And it's all your fault."

Robert laughed. "Are you trying to tell me you're normal?" he asked.

Something about the way he said "normal"

made it sound incredibly dull. I stared out at the lake for a moment. It was easy to see why it was called Misty Lake; a thin fog floated just above the surface, as it did almost every night. Moonlight seemed to tangle in the tendrils of the mist. It looked strange and mysterious.

"Well, I may not be normal," I said at last. "But if I have to be weird, I'd rather do it my own way."

"That makes sense," said Robert, somewhat to my astonishment.

"Were you weird?" I asked.

"Still am!" he cried gleefully, floating into the air.

"What are you doing here, anyway?" I said. "Aren't ghosts supposed to be restless spirits, trying to settle something? You know—you have to find the person who killed you, or locate your missing skull, or something like that?"

Robert laughed. "The only reason I'm here is to have a good time. I'll have to move on someday. But I'm in no hurry. What's time to a ghost?"

"But why are you *here*-here?" I said. "I mean, why haunt this particular place? Did you die here?"

"No, I *lived* here," he said. "By that I mean this is where I was happiest when I was alive. I was a counselor here the first time this place was used for a camp. Of course, it wasn't Camp Haunted Hills then. It was Camp Haw N'ted Hee Las. They didn't start calling this area the Haunted Hills until I came back from the dead to liven things up."

"How did you die?" I asked.

"That is a very personal question," said Robert as he slowly faded from sight. There's nothing worse than a testy ghost.

To my relief—I guess—Robert finally showed up the next day in my special effects class.

Harry was just getting ready to announce his big surprise to the rest of the special-effects class. I knew about it, of course, already. "Listen everyone," he cried, "I've got big news."

"Did he say he's got a big nose?" asked Robert, popping into view next to Harry and pointing to his oversize schnozz. I snorted, then instantly felt disloyal. I wondered how you make a ghost shut up.

"Well, what is it?" asked Keith.

"We're going to make a movie," said Harry triumphantly. "A *real* movie—well, not a movie-theater movie. But a movie that might be seen by millions of people."

He waited a moment for that statement to sink in.

"Well, tell us all about it!" said Brenda finally.

"Oh, do!" cried Robert. "I'm all atwitter." His features blurred as he started to vibrate, which was a trick I hadn't seen before.

Harry smiled. "I assume you're all familiar with *Worlds of Wonder.*"

"We'd have to live in a cave *not* to be," said Lucius. Which was rude but true. Gregory Stevens's decision to produce a weekly television show had gotten the kind of news coverage usually saved for a presidential election.

"Well, Gregory still has room in next season's schedule for a few new shows. So I pitched him a couple of ideas a few weeks ago. He asked me to develop one of them." Harry paused for effect. "Yesterday he called to give me the green light. And guess what? He wants it to be a Camp Haunted Hills project. No outsiders—staff and campers do the whole thing."

You could feel the excitement building in the room. Making a film for *WOW* was more than any of us would have dreamed about. Well, actually I'd had daydreams like that. But they weren't the kinds you expected to come true.

"What's the film about?" asked Keith.

Harry put a finger beside his beaky nose and smiled. "The topic is part of the genius of this idea," he said. "Think for a minute. What's the most logical subject for a group of fantasy film-makers living in the Oregon woods?"

"Sasquatch!" yelled Brenda.

"What's that?" asked Murky Jones, one of the older kids in the class. "Some kind of vegetable?"

Harry smiled. "Actually, it's the great hairy creature of the northwest forests," he said. "You've probably heard of it as Bigfoot. *Sasquatch* comes from an Indian name for the creatures. It means wild man of the woods. People have claimed to have seen them in California and Oregon for over a hundred and fifty years. They're supposed to be huge, manlike creatures, seven to eight feet tall, and covered with dark fur."

"And they have great big feet," said Keith Jackson.

"Which is how they got their other name," said Harry. "Myself, I prefer the Indian term. That's why my story is called 'Cry of the Sasquatch.' "

He looked around the room.

"So," he said. "Who wants to help make a movie?"

My hand shot up so fast I almost sprained my back.

Chapter Eleven

Volunteer Bigfoot

By the end of the day "Operation Bigfoot" was like a snowball rolling down a mountainside. The more people found out about it, the more they wanted to be involved.

"The magic of Gregory Stevens," said Harry that evening. "When I just wanted to have the effects class make a film for practice, no one wanted to help. Now I have to beat them off with a stick."

"He should be grateful," said Robert, who was standing on top of Harry's head. "It's probably the first time in his life he's been popular."

"What are you going to do?" I asked.

"Take the best and leave the rest," he said with a shrug.

"My, aren't we picky?" said Robert, stepping off Harry's head and floating down beside him. He made a face at Myron, who was resting on Harry's shoulder.

"Makes sense," I said, trying to squelch Robert while I answered Harry. "If Mr. Stevens really might use this film on *WOW*, you have to make it as good as you possibly can."

Suddenly I wondered if I would get to work on the film myself. My answer came the next day, when Harry started bringing in the other staff members who were going to help.

To my surprise, the first two who showed up were Dan and Aurora. Harry introduced them to the kids who didn't know them personally and explained that Dan was going to act in the film, taking the one part too old for a camper to play. Aurora, of course, would be in charge of makeup.

"Makeup and special effects often overlap," said Aurora, who was wearing spiked pink hair that morning. "For example, if you want to shoot a scene where someone ages right before your eyes that's a special effect. But the aging is done with makeup. Like this!"

She opened her kit and started applying makeup. It was incredible. Stopping every thirty seconds or so to explain what she was doing, she transformed herself from a beautiful young woman into an old hag in about fifteen minutes. It was like watching someone go through a whole lifetime in a quarter of an hour.

"Yech," said Robert when she was done. "I'm glad I died young."

Someone knocked at the door. Wrapping a shawl around her shoulders, Aurora hobbled over to open it. You would have sworn she was a hundred years old.

A tall, dark-haired man stepped into the room. "Hi, sweetheart," he said, bending down and giving Aurora a kiss on the cheek. "You look a little tired this morning."

I glanced at Dan. His cheeks were bright red. But he had no cause to worry. Aurora looked the guy right in the face and said, "Keep your lips to yourself, smart guy."

He laughed and strolled over to Harry. "You going to introduce me, or do I have to do it my-self?"

"This is Flash Milligan," said Harry. "He'll be in charge of lighting."

"He's gorgeous!" whispered Brenda.

I'm no expert on that kind of thing, but I guess when you get right down to it, Flash was as hand-some as Harry was homely. He had curly dark hair that tumbled over his forehead, big brown eyes, and a straight nose that was just the right size for his face. He was tall and lean, with broad shoulders and muscular arms.

Unfortunately, he didn't act the way he looked.

"Let's get one thing straight," he said, shoving aside some carefully arranged tools and sitting on the edge of our table. "I'm only working in this dump because I owe Greg Stevens a favor. I'll give you the best lighting I can—and that's the best available, because I'm as good as anyone in the field. But don't come running to me to wipe your nose or tie your shoes, because I don't particularly like kids, or camps, or corny science-fiction movies."

He looked around, then flashed us a dazzling smile. "Remember that, and we'll get along just fine." He stood up and headed for the door. "See you the first day of filming," he said just before he disappeared.

"What a jerk," said Lucius.

That was a laugh. Other than the fact that he was a lot better looking, I figured Flash was a perfect example of what Lucius would be like when he grew up.

"Well," said Aurora, "now that we've lived through that little unpleasantness, I want to start working on the film itself. So—I'll need someone to be a Sasquatch."

She looked around the room.

No one volunteered.

Suddenly Robert appeared in front of me. "Hey, Stuart!" he yelled, poking his fingers at my face the way Moe does to Curly in *The Three Stooges*. I knew perfectly well his fingers would go right through me without hurting, but I yelled and jumped up, anyway.

"Thank you, Stuart," said Aurora. "I think you'll make a very good Sasquatch."

"Me, too," gasped Robert, who was lying on the floor, holding his sides and laughing hysterically.

Just what I always wanted—a chance to play a walking fur factory. I bent down and pretended to tie my shoe. "I'll get you for this," I hissed.

"You'll have to catch me first!" said Robert. Then he vanished.

I remembered the obedience school where we had sent Jeremiah, our golden retriever, and wondered if they had something like that for ghosts.

Chapter Twelve

Into the Wilderness

"This is two you owe me," said Robert, leaning over my shoulder.

I groaned.

It was the first day of the third week of camp, and we were being bounced over an overgrown dirt road in a beat-up old Jeep. Harry was at the wheel, humming "My Way" through his nose.

"Watch out!" he yelled, too late to do me any good. We hit an enormous bump. I smacked my head on the roof and felt my spine jar as my rear end reconnected with the seat.

"Let's do it again!" cried Robert.

Pretending I was looking behind me to see how the others were doing, I turned to shush him.

Our caravan consisted of four vehicles: two Jeeps, a truck, and a van. We were heading into the woods because Gregory Stevens had called and told Harry he wanted genuine location shots for the Sasquatch movie. Peter Flinches sent out a scouting party, which found a perfect spot for filming—a spectacular cliff and falls several miles from the camp.

"Spectacular is right," said Aurora a few hours later. She shrugged out of her backpack and stared up at the falls. "It's gorgeous."

"Very romantic," said Flash Milligan, putting his arm around her waist.

"You need a good man for romance," replied Aurora, slipping neatly out of his hold. She picked up her backpack and walked off.

Someone sighed behind me. I figured it was Dan, but when I turned I saw Harry staring after Aurora. I hoped *he* wasn't getting a crush on her, too. Life around there was silly enough already.

Our campsite was about a mile from the falls, which was as close as we could get with most of the vehicles. Flash and Harry stayed at the cliff to discuss camera angles and lighting problems. The rest of us hiked back to set up the tents. When we were about halfway there Brenda grabbed my arm. "What's that?" she asked.

"What's what?" I asked. Then I heard it myself— a rustling in the leaves off to our left. At the same time I was hit by a powerful smell, a little like wet dog but not as unpleasant.

I stared into the woods. The underbrush was too thick; all I could see were leaves.

"Probably a raccoon," I said.

"Or a bear," added Robert cheerfully.

Between traveling and setting up, there was no time to film that day. We built a couple of fires and the people in charge of cooking made a terrific chicken dinner, with apple pie for dessert! After cleanup we began to plan the next day's shooting.

There were twenty of us in all. For a number of reasons, all of which seemed pretty stupid to me, the campers chosen for location work were mostly older kids. That was why Robert claimed I owed him. If he hadn't tricked me into letting Aurora turn me into a Sasquatch, I might be back at the main camp, fuming because I wasn't part of the trip. The only other kids my age were Brenda, who had come to help Aurora, and Lucius, who had a special genius for worming his way into things.

"How about a story?" said one of the older kids, as darkness fell.

"Stor-y, stor-y!" chanted several others.

"Okay, okay, I'll give you a story," said Dan, walking to the center of the circle we had made around the main fire. I remembered he was an actor. It made sense he would be a good storyteller. And this was a perfect chance to show off for Aurora.

If you like being scared, it was wonderful. While the stars winked into sight above us, Dan wove an eerie story about a man who wandered into a forest haunted by evil spirits.

Robert was sitting next to me. I was afraid he would start wisecracking and ruin the story. To my surprise, he became totally involved in it.

"I love a good ghost story," he said when it was over.

So do I. But I wasn't sure I liked them *that* good. I wondered if I would be able to sleep that night. I got so wrapped up thinking about the story that when someone tapped me on the shoulder, I almost jumped out of my skin.

It was Harry. He put a finger to his lips and motioned for me to follow him. Slipping away from the fire, I trailed him into the woods.

"What's up?" I asked when we were far enough away that no one could hear us.

"Let's have some fun," he whispered. His eyes sparkled behind the thick glasses.

I followed him to the back of the vehicles. I watched as he unlocked the van.

Once the doors were open, he pointed his flashlight at a large wooden box, held shut by a padlock. "The holo-projector," he whispered.

Instantly I knew what he had in mind.

"I smell mischief," sang Robert happily. He watched in approval as I helped Harry lift the projector from its box. At Harry's direction I went to get a large leather case sitting nearby. I knelt down and slipped the strap over my shoulder. When I tried to stand I almost fell over sideways. I wondered if I would make it to wherever we were going.

"Heavy!" I mouthed, without actually pronouncing the word.

"Battery," replied Harry in the same fashion.

We made it out of the van without any serious noise. A soft wind whispered through the night, thick with the smell of leaves, water, mold, and that strange, doglike odor I had noticed earlier.

I looked up. The sky was so black I saw thousands of stars I had never known existed.

Harry led me to a tree. Together we hoisted the projector and battery into the branches.

"Ready?" whispered Harry as he connected the last wire.

I looked down into the campsite. People were sitting in groups of threes and fours, talking quietly. A few kids were toasting marshmallows. Lucius was picking his nose, and Flash was trying to put his arm around Aurora. I figured this was as good a time as any.

"Ready," I whispered.

Harry flipped a switch. Myron-the-Dragon appeared about twenty feet from the campfire.

"Cute," said Robert. "But a trifle tiny, don't you think?"

"Let's skip levels two and three," said Harry, almost as though he had heard Robert. I heard the machine click as he moved the dial.

Imagine you're lazing beside a campfire. Suddenly you hear people shouting. You look up and see a sixteen-foot dragon slithering toward you. It has wings. Its skin is bright red. Its eyes glitter. Smoke is curling out of its nostrils.

The place exploded with screams and shouts. Robert began laughing so hard I think he would have fallen off our branch if he were alive. Lucius tried to climb a tree on the other side of the clearing. Flash was so panicked he tripped over a root and fell flat on his face.

Harry turned the dial again. "I made some adjustments yesterday," he said. "Let's see how she does as level five."

The dragon's size doubled again. It was so realistic even I was frightened! But the effect only lasted a few seconds before the image wavered and faded from sight. A few people began to laugh. Others shouted angrily. Flash Milligan moaned as he picked himself up.

And one more sound mingled with all those human noises. Off in the distance a strange cry—half howl, half sob—quivered into the night and hung there for what seemed an eternity.

Chapter Thirteen

I Get to Be a Star

Nobody got much sleep that night.

First we needed a couple of hours to quiet everyone down. Then there were endless questions about the holo-projector. Finally, just as we were heading for our tents, that strange howl trembled through the air again.

"Wolf?" asked Brenda nervously.

"No, boogie man!" said Flash. He had given himself a black eye when he tripped and he was in such a bad mood I would have been surprised to see him smile again before Thanksgiving.

The final disruption came after we were all asleep. At least, nearly all of us were. It started when I heard something scratching on my tent. I opened my eyes, but it was so dark I couldn't have seen my own nose, even if it was as big as Harry's. I closed my eyes.

I heard it again.

Skritch. *Skritch, Skritch.*

I rolled over and tried to go back to sleep. *Just a branch*, I thought.

After a moment of silence, the scratching started again, louder than ever. I fumbled in my sleeping bag for my flashlight, flicked it on, pointed it straight up, and saw a dark figure bending over the tent, scratching at the surface.

I'm sorry, but there are limits to my bravery. I let out a bellow that probably woke the light sleepers in California. It certainly woke everyone in the camp. More confusion as flashlights blinked on and people started stumbling out of their tents.

And what did they find? Lucius Colton, standing beside my tent, laughing hysterically.

"Not so brave now, are you Glassman?" He chuckled.

Flash, Dan, and Aurora informed Lucius that his timing was dumb and that they wanted everyone— and they meant *everyone*—to get their butts into bed.

While we were standing there shivering, I smelled that wet dog odor again. Suddenly I heard something moving in the bushes. Pointing with my flashlight, I saw the glint of an eye and a patch of dark fur.

"Look!" I cried.

But whatever it was had vanished, and I got

yelled at for causing more trouble. I tried to explain, but it was hopeless. Everyone was tired of jokes and false alarms. All they wanted was sleep.

At first I was too wound up to sleep myself. When I finally did conk out, it seemed as if only minutes had passed before I heard Aurora rustling the tent flaps and telling everyone to get up. I stumbled out and headed for the makeshift latrine on the west side of the camp, where I found a little patch of coarse black fur on one of the ropes holding the tarp in place.

I was not a happy camper.

I headed back to show the fur to Harry, figuring he was the only one likely to believe me. But Aurora caught me first. "Time to get started, Stuart," she said cheerfully.

I sighed. Aurora had warned me that my Sasquatch makeup would take several hours. "There will be no zippers or seams in this film!" Harry had declared, and Aurora felt the same way. I respected that. But I wasn't thrilled about sitting still for three or four hours of makeup.

Aurora had set up shop behind the van. She started by gluing pieces of plastic onto my cheeks and brow, to change the contours of my face.

Someone brought a plate of eggs, and Brenda fed me while Aurora worked on my hands. Every once in a while she held up a mirror so I could see how

it was coming. It was a little scary to see myself disappearing and a small Sasquatch starting to take my place.

"I did a lot of research for this," said Aurora. "It's based on the most respected sightings and photographs. If the Sasquatch really exist, this is what they look like."

Robert popped up now and then while this was going on, but he seemed to find it pretty boring—especially since I kept closing my eyes so he couldn't trick me into laughing by making funny faces or rude gestures.

"This is too dull for me," he said. "I'll see you later."

I nodded slightly.

"Don't move!" said Aurora.

It was almost noon before she was ready to let the rest of the crew see me. When I shambled around the edge of the van, everyone turned and stared. For a moment no one said a word. Then they began to applaud. I felt wonderful, even though I had had nothing to do with it.

"I guess they like it," said Brenda.

"Mmmphh-oh," I replied, which was as close as I could get to "Guess so" with all the plastic I had glued to my face.

The makeup time hadn't been wasted, because

the rest of the crew had been setting up cameras and equipment out by the falls. Harry planned to start by filming a scene where Dan, who was sort of the hero of the story, found a young Bigfoot—namely me—who was wounded and unable to walk.

While we were filming, I got a creepy feeling that someone outside our group was watching me. Of course, I couldn't explain that to anyone, because I couldn't talk. All I could do was nod and grunt, or write notes on a pad if I really wanted to say something. That wasn't the kind of thing I could have put down on a note.

I should have tried, anyway.

Brenda and Aurora made sure I had plenty to drink. That was good, since a day in that costume was like a week in the jungle. By three o'clock I smelled like a wet dog myself.

Not that they overworked me. One of the first things I learned about filmmaking is this: if you're an actor, you spend most of your time waiting. It seemed like forever while they set up camera angles and measured light and checked sound. Fortunately, someone had brought a beach umbrella. I spent a lot of time napping in the shade by the edge of the water, which was a relief after all the sleep I had missed the night before.

About four-thirty Harry came over and sat down beside me. "I want to do the farewell scene at sunset," he said. "Can you hold out that long?"

I nodded. It wasn't pleasant being in that outfit. But I had spent most of the day just lying around, so I figured I could manage.

"Thanks," said Harry, squeezing my shoulder. I felt glad I had said yes.

The crew decided to take a break and go back to the campsite for dinner. It was hard for me to walk in my costume—the big feet kept catching on things—so they carried me on a stretcher. I felt like royalty.

Of course, I didn't eat like royalty, since I had to have my supper through a straw. Robert appeared next to me and called me a real "sucker." I checked to make sure no one was looking, then wrote him a rude note. Just as I was putting in the exclamation points, a seven-foot-tall creature covered with fur ran out of the trees, snatched me up, and carried me off into the forest.

Chapter Fourteen

Night Journey

The arm that held me was enormous. I screamed for help, but my face was pressed into thick black fur. The wet dog smell was overwhelming.

When the creature grabbed me, I was so terrified my heart nearly stopped. I think I went into shock, because for a while everything seemed to be happening in a dream. I remember the creature shifting me from arm to arm. I remember the forest streaking by in patches of light and dark green, lit by the setting sun. I remember smashing through thick patches of undergrowth and splashing through swift, gurgling streams. I began to be thankful for the heavy costume, which protected me from the lashing branches.

Finally the creature carried me into a dark cave. *This is it*, I thought. *I'll never see my mother and father again.*

It was so dark I couldn't see a thing—not even

the monster beside me. I started to cry. I was shaking with terror.

I kept waiting for something awful to happen. When it didn't, I calmed down and began to think a little more clearly. And the first thing I thought of was what I had heard as I was being carried off: "Harry, you two are a riot. This is even better than last night."

My heart sank as I realized that the rest of the crew thought this was another Camp Haunted Hills joke! I knew from experience that the more Harry protested he had nothing to do with it, the less they would believe him.

My gloomy thoughts were interrupted by a burst of grunts and snorts from just outside the cave. Whatever had captured me picked me up and carried me back outside.

Three more creatures were waiting in the moonlight. I began to shake again.

I stand just over five feet high. These creatures were at least seven feet tall. The biggest was probably close to eight. Their bodies were covered with thick black fur. They had broad chests and powerful arms. Their feet were enormous.

I had just been kidnapped by a band of Sasquatch!

As I studied them, I realized what a good job Aurora had done on my makeup. I looked exactly

83

like them—or more precisely, like one of their kids. Suddenly I realized what was going on: The Bigfeet thought I was real!

I wanted to take off my costume. But I couldn't. Aurora and Harry were so concerned with making it appear authentic that I had been sewn into it.

I decided maybe it was just as well. Who knows what the Sasquatch might do if I revealed myself as a human?

The tallest creature bent down and began to sniff at me. He made a puzzled sound. I suppose I didn't smell like a Sasquatch. But by the that time I probably didn't smell much like a human, either.

The one who had captured me bent down and looked me in the eyes. Her face was strange and hairy. *But her eyes were human.* I don't know— maybe that's the wrong word. But I was sure the creature looking at me was intelligent.

She made some sounds. Did they have a language? I wondered what she might be saying. Was she telling me her name? Was she asking how I had gotten lost? Suddenly I realized that not only did they think I was a young Sasquatch, they probably thought they had *rescued* me from the humans.

I tried to say something, but the plastic Aurora had glued to my face made it impossible. The words came out a garbled mess. The female Bigfoot looked at me sadly. I wondered if she thought I was retarded.

Just then Robert showed up. "Boy, were you hard to find," he said. "I've been looking everywhere for you."

I growled at him. He laughed and shook his head. "Sounds like your new playmates are wearing off on you. Who are they anyway?"

"Robert," I said, "get me out of this mess." Actually, that was what I *tried* to say. What came out was "Mmphh, guh ee owwwf thh mff."

The female Bigfoot patted my head.

"Well, don't worry," said Robert. I'll get you out of this."

"You'd better," I said, in the same garbled fashion. "You got me into it!"

Which was true. If he hadn't tricked me into volunteering to be a Sasquatch, I would have been back in camp right now, instead of standing here in the wilderness with a gang of eight-foot tall monsters sniffing my armpits.

"Sorry," said Robert. I can't understand a word you're saying. See you soon!"

He vanished, leaving me alone with the Sasquatch.

Chapter Fifteen

Me and My Big Feet

The tallest of the Sasquatch tipped back his head and howled. I recognized the sound from the night before.

This time it was slightly different, with a waver in the middle and a little yodel at the end. I wondered if it was because a different Bigfoot was making the sound, or if the howls carried messages, and so changed according to meaning.

I decided the second idea was right, because soon several more Sasquatch arrived, as if they had been called.

It was awesome to see them come creeping into the clearing. First I would hear a slight rustling. Then, if the angle was right, I would catch a glint of moonlight from a pair of eyes high above the ground. Then the great, hairy creature itself would shamble out of the forest, making strange, throaty noises. I was sure they were all asking about me.

I wondered what they planned to do with me.

Over a dozen Sasquatch gathered in the clearing. I felt *very* small. With only the moon for light I couldn't tell them all apart. But I had managed to get a sense for the first four. The biggest, who was clearly in charge of the tribe, I named Big Boss. The female who had captured me seemed to be his mate. I decided to call her Momma B. Since the other two seemed to be part of the family, I named them after my father's brothers: Uncle David and Uncle Byron.

After a while Momma B took me back into the cave. She positioned herself in front of the exit so I couldn't escape. Outside, I could hear the Sasquatch getting louder. They sounded angry.

"Probably trying to decide whether to bake you or fry you," said Robert, drifting down through the roof. The best thing about his arrival was the slight glow he cast. It brought a little relief from the darkness of the cave.

I noticed something white on the floor. My pad! I had been clutching it when Momma B first grabbed me. I suppose I had been too scared to drop it. Feeling around, I found the pencil nearby.

"What's going on?" I wrote. I printed in big block letters, since I couldn't hold the pencil the way I normally would.

Robert shrugged. "Things look pretty sticky. When I first got back to camp I heard Harry call the main camp on the CB radio. He got hold of Peter Flinches and confirmed that this was no prank. Peter is sending reinforcements. In the meantime, the crew split into three groups to search for you. They left Brenda in the van with the CB radio to act as a communication center. I guess they figured she'd be safe as long as it was locked."

"Did you tell her where I am?" I wrote.

"How?"

I couldn't believe him. "The same way you tell me things!" I wrote.

"Are you kidding? I already told you, I don't like having more than one mortal in my life at one time. It's like having two girlfriends. It makes things too complicated."

I remembered him saying that. I also remembered thinking his real reason was the fewer people who knew about him, the more practical jokes he could play on me. Under the circumstances, it didn't seem like a good enough reason to keep quiet.

I picked up the pad and wrote "ROBERT!!!"— hoping the exclamation points would show my feelings.

"Oh, all right," he said sulkily. "I'll go talk to her. But only because it's for you! Of course, I'm not sure how she's going to take it."

He leaned back against the cave wall and put one hand around his knee. "I mean, it could be pretty bad. Picture poor Brenda, locked in that van. It's the middle of the night. She's all alone, everyone else is off hunting for the monsters that kidnapped her friend. Then all of a sudden *I* show up."

He shook his head. "I don't know. Doesn't sound to me like a good way to have your first encounter with a ghost. She'll probably faint. Or maybe she'll just go clear out of her mind. I mean, that's an awfully small space to come face-to-face with a ghost—if you're not used to it."

"Then go find Harry!" I wrote.

"That might be a good idea," said Robert. "Of course, I don't have any idea where he is. It could take awhile."

I figured that was baloney. He probably had special powers, or contacts in the spirit world, or something that would let him locate Harry easily. I was trying to figure out how to write that down when we heard a commotion outside. I scrambled to the front of the cave. But Momma B caught me and held me against her so I couldn't see what was going on.

I heard voices, both Bigfoot and human, and lots of shouting and screaming. Then a sound like rocks smashing together. Then a lot of howling, and a sound I couldn't identify at first but finally recognized as the noise of gigantic feet slapping against the ground.

I wasn't sure, but it sounded like a victory celebration.

Chapter Sixteen

Brenda Breaks Through

"Well, you can forget about Harry," said Robert a few minutes later. We were sitting back in the cave, where Momma B shooed me after the hubbub died down.

"Wahaw hoppn?" I said.

"You want to know what happened?" asked Robert.

I nodded.

"As near as I can make out, Harry and Aurora and four or five others came stumbling into the camp." He smiled. "That Harry's a nice guy. But he'll never be a soldier—"

I made an impatient sound. Robert got the idea.

"Anyway, once they were here, it was too late to turn around. Your furry friends chased them into the cave on the other side of the clearing, then piled rocks in front of it. They didn't completely block it off. But it only takes one Bigfoot to guard it. He's just sitting there with a stick, and anyone who pokes his head out is apt to lose it. Once that was taken care of, the Sasquatch had a victory dance. Too bad you missed it. It was like something out of *National Geographic*."

I groaned. Now what were we going to do?

"Maybe I'd better get Brenda after all," said Robert.

I shook my head. As silly as it was, his speech had convinced me that sending him for Brenda was a bad idea.

"Well, I'm going to go scout around," he said. "I'll be back in a while."

I nodded glumly and watched him disappear. A few minutes later the female Sasquatch crawled back into the cave and picked me up. I struggled to get loose at first, but she held me tight. Then she sat down and began rocking back and forth, making a strange noise in her throat. I'm not sure, but I think it was a lullaby.

I decided to relax and enjoy it. I mean, I sure wasn't going anywhere. I was exhausted. The night had gotten cold, and Momma B was big and warm. But just as I was starting to drift off, I heard a familiar voice say, "You'd better stay on your toes if you want to get out of this mess."

He was right. While I was drifting off, Momma B had done the same thing. Her big head drooped to one side. Here eyes were closed. Her breathing was slow and even.

It was definitely time to get going. I crawled to the front of the cave. Unfortunately, Uncle David and Uncle Byron were squatting on either side of the entrance, wide-awake.

Having an eight-foot-tall pile of fur growl at you is not a happy experience. I scrambled back into the cave.

"Crossing guard in a bad mood?" asked Robert.

I growled at him. I was starting to feel like a Bigfoot myself.

"What now?" asked Robert.

I picked up the pad and wrote, "THINK!!!" Then I settled down and tried to do the same thing myself. I hadn't been at it for more than ten minutes when I heard another disturbance outside. I crawled to the front of the cave and was astonished to see the camp van come bouncing through the trees. Whoever was driving was leaning on the horn. Honking it for all it was worth.

The Big Boss stood in the middle of the clearing, howling and bellowing. The other Sasquatch were jumping up and down. Uncle David and Uncle Byron were on their feet, baring their teeth and hissing at the van.

I tried slipping out of the cave, but they spotted me before I had gone three feet. Uncle David picked me up and put me down inside the cave.

I crawled in far enough to satisfy him—but not so far that I couldn't see what was going on. Momma B had woken up. She put her arm around me and pulled me against her side. I realized she was trying to protect me. She probably thought the humans were going to steal me again!

The van stopped in the middle of the clearing. I could see Brenda in the driver's seat. She looked terrified. I didn't blame her. I figured she thought when she came roaring into the Sasquatch camp, horn blaring and headlights blazing, the beasts would run off. How could she know they thought they were protecting one of their own?

What a fine mess this was: Harry and Aurora trapped on one side of the clearing, me here, and Brenda stuck in the van. The van! Suddenly I had what was probably the most brilliant idea of my life.

I squirmed out of Big Momma B's grasp. She made a noise, but when she saw I was heading toward the back of the cave she decided it was all right.

I found my pad: "Need a distraction," I wrote. "Have to get into van."

"Hey, babe," said Robert. "No problemo. Let's see what Bigfeet do when they see a ghost."

Chapter Seventeen

Myron's Turn

Momma B was at the front of the cave with Uncle David and Uncle Byron.

When they saw me moving toward them they got very wary. I had the feeling they throught I had been polluted by the humans and had to be kept away from them or I would want to go back—like a country kid who's had a taste of the big city.

I leaned against the cave and whimpered, trying to sound tired and bored. They relaxed a bit.

Just then, Robert burst into view on the other side of the clearing, howling like a fire engine.

I don't know how he was able to decide when they could see him, but obviously he had that ability. The Sasquatch turned around, took one look at him, and went bananas.

I took advantage of the confusion to shoot across the clearing to the van. I stumbled over my feet twice and actually fell down once. But I made it.

Except that when I pounded on the door, Brenda, screamed and cowered back.

"Bwwma!" I yelled. "Ishme! Stoo! Lemmin!"—which was as close as I could get to "Brenda, it's me, Stuart. Let me in!"

She just checked the locks to make sure they were tight.

I reached up and ripped off the piece of latex and fur glued to my forehead. I felt as if several inches of skin went with it, but Brenda got the message. She opened the door.

"Stuart," she said as I scrambled into the van, "thank goodness it's you. What are we going to do?"

I pointed to my mouth and mumbled.

"Right," she said. "You can't talk. Wait a minute."

She checked the locks again, then went to the rear of the van. After a minute she came back with the makeup box. Opening it, she took out a bottle of clear liquid. She started swabbing it on the pieces of latex and fur glued around my mouth and hands. A minute later I could pull them off without it feeling like major surgery. What a relief!

"How did you get here?" I asked, when my mouth was clear.

"Harry directed me by walkie-talkie. The idea

terrified me. But we thought if I drove in making plenty of noise, the Sasquatch would run. Everyone claims they're very shy."

"They probably are," I said. "But these guys were trying to protect me."

"Something about you, Stuart," said Robert, who had materialized in the driver's seat. "People just want to take care of you."

"Shut up," I said, not caring if Brenda thought I was crazy or not. Then I worried she might think I was talking to her, so I added, "Not you. Him."

"What are you talking about?"

"Nothing. It's been a long day. If I talk funny just ignore me."

I must have sounded totally insane. But I couldn't think of anything else to say—especially since I knew I was going to have to talk to Robert again before this was all over.

I went to the back of the van, hoping the box I wanted would be there.

It was. Unfortunately, it was locked. I started looking around for something to attack the box with. Suddenly I remembered where the tools were. I pulled open a door in the floor of the van. The tire iron was nestled in beside the spare. It was perfect: a long metal rod with a tapered end for prying off hubcaps.

I grabbed it.

"Stuart!" yelled Brenda, "you're not going to try to fight them, are you?"

"Of course not," I said. "One of them wants to be my mother. Stand back."

I inserted the tapered end of the tire iron under the latch and wrenched outward. The latch flew off and hit the far wall of the van.

"Very nice," said Robert. "I didn't know you had it in you."

I lifted the lid and heaved a sigh of relief. The holo-projector was inside.

I grabbed the battery pack and started connecting the wires to the projector.

"What are you doing?" asked Brenda.

"Watch!" I said. I looked past her to Robert. "I need another diversion—long enough for me to get up on the roof of the van."

"You got it, boss," he said. He gave me the thumbs-up sign and floated out through the roof.

Brenda looked frightened. "I'll do what I can," she said.

"Thanks," I answered, not realizing what she meant. I picked up the projector and stationed myself by the door, waiting for Robert to distract the Sasquatch. Several of them stood near the van, eyeing it cautiously. I unlocked the door and grabbed the handle.

"Now!" I yelled.

"Okay!" said Brenda. To my astonishment, she opened the other door and ran into the clearing. "Watch out, you big jerks," she shouted. "Here comes Brenda!"

"Brenda, come back!" I yelled.

"What's she doing?" asked Robert, who was sitting on top of the van waiting for me.

"Your job," I snapped. "Providing a distraction!"

I braced my foot on the window as I spoke, hoping the Sasquatch would keep their eyes on Brenda long enough for me to do what I had to do. I put the projector on the roof, then scrambled up after it.

"Stuart!" yelled Brenda. "Do something!"

I looked out at the clearing in time to see one of the Sasquatch snatch her up and head for the cave. Several others began running toward the van.

I braced the projector between my legs and turned it on.

Nothing happened.

One of the Sasquatch was climbing onto the roof.

"Do something!" I yelled at Robert.

"BOO!" he said, making himself visible to the Sasquatch.

It jumped backward and tumbled off the hood. Unfortunately, its reaction seemed to come from surprise, not from fear of ghosts. He started climbing up again immediately.

"Well, I'm just abashed," said Robert. "Usually I'm much more effective."

"It was good enough," I said, suddenly remembering the last thing I needed to do. I flipped a switch on the left side of the holo-projector. Instantly Myron appeared at the edge of the clearing, complete with wings and smoking nose. I rolled the dial. The small dragon disappeared. In its place was a sixteen-foot monster. Trying to remember the sequence of Myron's movements, I turned the projector this way and that.

The dragon slithered into the clearing.

The Sasquatch began to howl. They gathered together in a clump. They were frightened. But they weren't running.

"Stuart!" cried a voice from the far side of the clearing. "I worked on it again this morning! Try level five!"

"It's all or nothing, kid," said Robert.

I turned the dial.

It was magnificent. Myron's image didn't merely double, it tripled. He was incredible—a bright red, three-dimensional, fifty-foot-long, smoke-breathing, tail-lashing monster so real he looked as if he had escaped from the nearest nightmare.

It was too much for the Sasquatch. They dropped Brenda and ran into the woods.

All except for Momma Bigfoot. She ran toward the van.

"She wants to save you," whispered Robert. I could tell by his voice that he was impressed by her courage.

It broke my heart to do it, but I stuck my face over the edge of the van. When she saw my human features poking out from the furry costume, she cried out in shock. The look on her face was a terrible mixture of sorrow and betrayal.

She whimpered, then turned and slowly followed the others into the forest.

A lump seemed to get stuck in my throat as I watched her go.

Chapter Eighteen

Closing Credits

"Well," said Harry as the van bounced along the rutty path back to our campsite, "that was definitely the most interesting day of my life."

"Mine, too," I said, peeling off another piece of latex.

It was almost dawn when we reached camp. The other search groups, one led by Dan and one by Flash, pulled in about a half an hour later. We greeted them with hot coffee and doughnuts.

"Everything's under control," said Harry. "Under control and in the can."

"What do you mean?" asked Flash.

Harry pulled out a Minicam. "A good filmmaker is always prepared," he said. "The lighting may not be the best—but, boy, have I got some exciting footage in here. I shot it from the cave."

The man was born to make movies.

Poor Lucius actually looked disappointed to see me. I don't think he wanted me dead or anything. But I don't think it would have bothered him if the Sasquatch had kept me for a week or two. Flash seemed to have the same feeling about Harry—especially since it was clear that Aurora was more interested in him than she was in either Flash or Dan.

"So what if he looks like a pelican," she told Brenda a few days later. "He has the most interesting ideas of anyone I know."

Brenda repeated that to me one night while we were sitting by the lake. I still don't want anyone to think she's my girlfriend, or anything stupid like that. But I figure anyone brave enough to run into the middle of a tribe of angry Sasquatch deserves a little respect now and then.

A week later the entire camp gathered in the mess hall to see a rough cut—that's movie talk for first draft—of "Cry of the Sasquatch." Harry had adapted the story, a little, to take in our adventures in the woods, and as I sat in the dark and watched Momma B, I felt that lump in my throat again. Even if she was seven feet tall and covered with fur, she was a good person.

As the lights came up, everyone applauded.

Gregory Stevens walked to the front of the room and held up his hands for silence.

"It's rough," he said. "But I think it will work." He looked around and smiled. "Congratulations," he yelled. "You're going to have a film on *Worlds of Wonder!*".

I jumped to my feet and threw my arms around Harry.

We were filmmakers!

Of course, as you well know, Harry went on to turn that short segment from *Worlds of Wonder* into one of the most successful motion pictures of all time.

But now you also know the true story of what happened that summer, including how, with the help of Robert and Brenda, I saved my friends from a band of furious Sasquatch.

"But wait," I can hear you say. "Those movies were just make-believe. There's no truth to them."

That's good. In fact, it's just what we wanted you to think. You see, after we talked it over, we decided that the best thing for the Sasquatch was for them to be left alone. So, unlike people who are always taking fake films and trying to pretend they're real, we decided to do the opposite. We took our real footage and pretended that it had all been done with special effects.

If we hadn't, who knows how many tourists, sightseers, and scientists would be hunting for Momma B and her family?

But, you're wondering, won't people start looking for them after they read this book? I don't think so.

After all you don't believe this story—do you?

About the Author and Illustrator

Bruce Coville has written over a dozen books for young readers, including Sarah's Unicorn and *The Monster's Ring*. He has also written three musical plays for young audiences. Mr. Coville was born in the central New York area where he has lived most of his life. Before becoming a full-time writer, he worked as a magazine editor, a teacher, a toy-maker, and a gravedigger. He is the author of the first Camp Haunted Hills book, *How I Survived My Summer Vacation*.

Tom Newsom was born in Texas and has been a freelance artist since his graduation from Art Center College. He has done many book covers for young readers, and his illustrations have appeared in such magazines as *Discover*, *Reader's Digest*, and *Field & Stream*.